A SERIES OF UNFORTUNATE EVENTS

SUPPLEMENTARY MATERIALS

Lemony Snicket

THE LUMP OF COAL

Art by Brett Helquist

 H

Printed in the U.S.A.
All rights reserved. No part of this book may be
used or reproduced in any manner whatsoever without
written permission except in the case of brief quotations
embodied in critical articles and reviews. For information
address HarperCollins Children's Books, a division of HarperCollins
Publishers, 1350 Avenue of the Americas, New York, NY 10019.
www.harpercollinschildrens.com

Library of Congress Cataloging-in-Publication Data
Snicket, Lemony.
The lump of coal / by Lemony Snicket ; art by Brett Helquist. —
1st ed.
p.   cm.
Summary: A lump of coal that wants to be an artist, but would settle for making decorative marks on a
piece of grilled meat, rolls out of a forgotten bag of charcoal one winter and rolls through town seeking a
miracle.
ISBN 978-0-06-157428-3 (trade bdg.) — ISBN 978-0-06-157425-2 (lib. bdg.)
[1. Coal—Ficion. 2. Miracles—Fiction. 3. Christmas—Fiction.] I. Helquist, Brett, ill. II. Title.
PZ7.S6795Lum 2008   2007041931
[Fic]—dc22   CIP
                                                                                                        AC

Book design by
Alison Donalty
1 3 5 7 9 10 8 6 4 2
❖ First Edition

THE LUMP OF COAL

The holiday season is a time for storytelling, and whether you are hearing the story of a candelabra staying lit for more than a week, or a baby born in a barn without proper medical supervision, these stories often feature miracles. Miracles are like pimples, because once you start looking for them you find more than you ever dreamed you'd see, and this holiday story features any number of miracles, depending on your point of view.

The story begins with a lump of coal, who for the sake of argument could think, talk, and move itself around. Like many people who dress in black, the lump of coal was interested in becoming an artist. The lump of coal dreamed of a miracle—that one day it would get to draw rough, black lines on a canvas or, more likely, on a breast of chicken or salmon filet by participating in a barbeque.

But barbeques, sadly, are for summer, and this is a holiday story and so takes place in the dead of winter, when the air is gray and wet shoes line up in the hallways, shivering and crying tears of sleet. It is difficult to find a barbeque in the winter, although it is easy to find small animals scurrying through backyards and tipping things over such as abandoned snow-covered lawn chairs, frozen birdbaths, and forgotten bags of charcoal, and this is how the small, flammable hero of our story found itself tumbling out into the world.

"This isn't the miracle I was hoping for," said the lump of coal, "but perhaps if I roll around a bit I can find something interesting."

The lump of coal rolled out of the backyard, taking care to avoid the inevitable puddles of winter, and soon found itself in the center of town. You would think that the center of town would be bustling during the holiday season, but most shoppers were bustling around at the mall several miles away, so there was plenty of room on the sidewalk for the lump of coal.

It window-shopped for a while, and then to its delight the lump of coal found itself outside an art gallery. In the window were several paintings that looked like someone had taken a dark, crumbly substance and smeared it all over a piece of paper.

"I can't believe it!" cried the lump of coal. "Here is an art gallery that displays art by lumps of coal! It's a miracle!"

When the lump of coal rolled inside, however, it discovered that the art gallery was not a miracle after all. "We do not represent artists such as yourself," said the gallery owner after the lump of coal had introduced itself. The gallery owner had a long, oily mustache and a strange accent that the lump of coal suspected was fake. "We have a wide selection of works by human beings that suits us just fine. Please go away, and don't leave smudges on my artistic floor."

Disappointed, the lump of coal rolled outside. "That wasn't the artistic opportunity I was hoping for," it said to itself. "But if I roll around a bit more, perhaps I can find something interesting."

The lump of coal rolled farther down the block, and stopped in front of a building where powerful smells were wafting, a phrase which here means "coming from nearby, even though the door was closed." A sign on the building informed passersby

that the building was named MR. WONG'S KOREAN BARBEQUE PALACE & SECRETARIAL SCHOOL, which made the lump of coal gasp in delight, because I forgot to tell you that for the sake of argument the lump of coal could read.

"It's a miracle!" cried the lump of coal, and certainly there was every reason to believe this was so. A Korean restaurant is an excellent opportunity to enjoy an indoor barbeque—in fact, many such establishments have small barbeque pits installed in the tables, so you can do the barbequing yourself. I have spent many pleasant evenings in Korean restaurants, taking shelter from the winter cold, warming myself by the barbeque pit at my table, and enjoying the smell of the toasted rice tea, eggplant salad, and pickled cabbage served alongside the roasted meats and vegetables.

When the lump of coal rolled inside, however, it discovered that Mr. Wong's Korean Barbeque Palace and Secretarial School was not a miracle after all. The air was filled with the smell of oregano, which is not a Korean spice, and the owner was wearing a pair of very ugly earrings and a rude scowl on her face. "I don't need any coal," she said. "I get all my coal from a Korean restaurant supply factory. Everything in this restaurant has to be one hundred percent Korean."

"But Wong isn't even a Korean name," the lump of coal said. "And judging by the smell, I don't think you're using proper Korean spices."

"Please go away," said the restaurant owner, "and don't leave smudges on my Korean floor."

The lump of coal did what it was told, and began to grow very despondent, a word which here means "certain that a miracle would not occur after all." "Perhaps miracles only happen to human beings," it said, "or maybe miracles are only as genuine as Mr. Wong's Korean Barbeque Palace and Secretarial School. Perhaps I should just bury myself and become a diamond after thousands of years of intense pressure."